The Thomas Augmented Reality animations have toolbars. Here's how to use the toolbar buttons.

Tap this to return to your home page.

Tap the camera to take a photo.

Tap this to open or close your toolbar.

Move the direction button up, down, right or left to steer Harold the Helicopter.

D0348975

Need some help?
If you've got a problem, check out our website:
www.carltonbooks.co.uk/icarltonbooks/thomas

THIS IS A CARLTON BOOK

Text and design © Carlton Books Limited 2015

Published in 2015 by Carlton Books Limited,
an imprint of the Carlton Publishing Group,
20 Mortimer Street, London W1T 3JW

A catalogue record for this book is available from the British Library.

HiT entertainment

CARLTON
KiDS

© 2015 HIT Entertainment Limited
Thomas & Friends ™

CREATED BY BRITT ALLCROFT

Based on the Railway Series by the Reverend W Awdry
© 2015 Gullane (Thomas) LLC.
Thomas the Tank Engine & Friends and Thomas & Friends
are trademarks of Gullane (Thomas) Limited.
Thomas the Tank Engine & Friends and Design is Reg. U.S.
Pat. & Tm. Off.

ISBN 978-1-78312-135-9
Printed in Dongguan, China

Writer: Emily Stead
Designer: Leanne Henricus

Thomas the Tank Engine is the Number 1 Engine on the Island of Sodor. He works hard each day and tries his best to be a **Really Useful Engine**. Sometimes he gets into scrapes, but help is never too far away. Let's follow Thomas as he visits his friends on Sodor.

"Follow me, I'm the leader!"

Join in with this fun railway rap!

Thomas has so many friends,
The list is long, it never ends,
James and Percy huff and puff,
And Emily, she knows her stuff.
Henry, Edward, what a pair!
Toby, like I say, he's square,
Gordon thunders down the line,
Everyone's a friend of mine!

AUGMENTED REALITY

See a lifesize Thomas appear in your room! Tap the screen to blow his whistle and make steam come out of his funnel!

BEST FRIENDS FOREVER!

Thomas and Percy are best friends. Percy arrived on the Island of Sodor when the big engines James, Gordon and Henry went on strike and wouldn't pull their trains. Percy was such a useful little engine that The Fat Controller asked Percy to stay and work on his Railway. Thomas was so pleased!

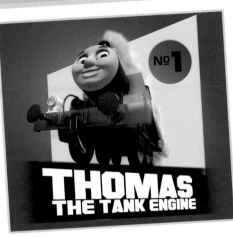

THOMAS
THE TANK ENGINE

NUMBER: 1
PAINTWORK: Blue with red boiler bands and buffer beam.
WHEELS: 6
FUEL: Thomas is a Steamie and runs on coal.

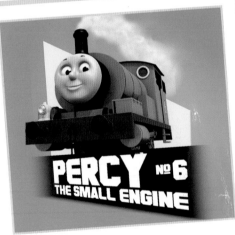

PERCY № 6
THE SMALL ENGINE

NUMBER: 6
PAINTWORK: Green with red boiler bands and buffer beam.
WHEELS: 4
FUEL: Coal makes Percy's firebox fizz and his pistons pump!

Snowy fun together!

When the day's work is done these cheeky little engines love to have adventures together!

Time to wake up, Percy!

Thomas and Rocky help their coal-dusted friend Percy.

BIG BUDDIES

The three big engines in the famous Steam Team are called Gordon, Henry and James. They are all strong and fast engines and really good friends!

HENRY
THE BIG ENGINE

№3

NUMBER: 3

PAINTWORK: Green with red boiler bands and a red buffer beam.

WHEELS: 10 and 6 on his tender.

FUEL: Coal, like the other Steamies.

Henry the Green Engine, steaming through the fog.

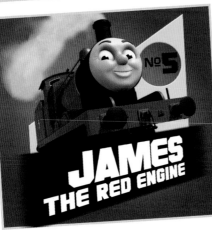

JAMES
THE RED ENGINE

NUMBER: 5

PAINTWORK: Splendid red with a gold dome and gold boiler bands.

WHEELS: 8 and 6 on his tender.

FUEL: Coal, but he doesn't like being covered in coal dust!

AUGMENTED REALITY

Tap on the buttons to meet the Steam Team and find out who their best friends are. Pinch and zoom to take a closer look!

Sometimes James is too big for his buffers!

GORDON
THE BIG ENGINE

NUMBER: 4

PAINTWORK: Blue with a bright red buffer beam.

WHEELS: 12 and 6 on his tender.

FUEL: Plenty of coal so he can reach top speeds.

Big blue Gordon is the longest and fastest engine on Sodor. His main job is to pull the Express. If Gordon is busy, helpful Henry sometimes takes Gordon's trains. James is a medium-sized engine who tries to keep up with his big friends. He is very proud of his bright red coat of paint. "Mind my paintwork!" you'll hear him shout.

THE STEAMWORKS TEAM

Head over to the Sodor Steamworks and there you'll find Victor and Kevin. It's their job to fix the Steamies that come to visit with a wonky whistle or a burst safety valve. Victor the steam engine is in charge and Kevin the yellow crane is his helper.

Clumsy Kevin always does his best!

VICTOR

PAINTWORK: Dark red with yellow boiler bands.

WHEELS: 4 – Victor is a Narrow Gauge Engine.

FUEL: Coal, like the other Steamies.

KEVIN THE CRANE

PAINTWORK: Yellow with yellow and black hazard stripes.

WHEELS: 4

FUEL: This little mobile crane runs on diesel.

Victor and Kevin fit new road wheels on Flynn the Fire Engine.

Busy Victor is brilliant at fixing steam engines.

Friendly Kevin is always ready to lend a helping hook, clumsily crashing about the place! Victor wisely tells Kevin to slow down and take his time, otherwise accidents can happen. Together they make a Really Useful team!

QUARRY CHUMS

Merrick and Owen spend all their days at the Blue Mountain Quarry. Perched high up on either side of the Quarry, they can see for miles! Owen is a traction engine who sends cargo cars full of slate up and down the Mountain. Merrick fills the Narrow Gauge Engines' slate trucks with a swing of his hook. "Lift and load!" calls mighty Merrick.

OWEN
THE TRACTION ENGINE

PAINTWORK: Orange and grey with an orange name plate.

WHEELS: None. He's based on a vertical traction boiler.

JOB: Pulls trucks of slate up and down the Quarry incline.

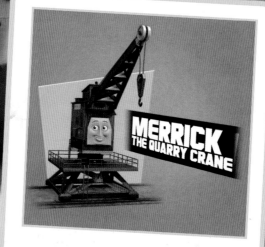

MERRICK
THE QUARRY CRANE

PAINTWORK: A red cab with a rusty brown crane arm.

WHEELS: He doesn't need any!

JOB: Swings heavy boulders down to the stone-cutting shed.

Thomas loves to make the trip across Blondin Bridge to hear all the latest news at the Quarry. Sometimes Thomas helps at the Quarry too, taking the trains of slate trucks to other parts of the Island.

CARRIAGE COUPLE

Annie and Clarabel are the most famous carriages on the Island of Sodor. They belong to Thomas and happily roll behind him up and down Thomas' branch line. Some people say that Annie and Clarabel are a little bit old-fashioned, but Thomas doesn't think so. He is very proud of both of his clever coaches!

Thomas and his carriages puff proudly along.

Annie and Clarabel love to explore the Island together.

Two happy coaches!

CLARABEL

PAINTWORK: Clarabel is brown and has her name painted on each side.

WHEELS: 4

FUEL: Carriages don't run on fuel – they need an engine to pull them!

ANNIE

PAINTWORK: Just like Clarabel, Annie is brown and has her name painted in white.

WHEELS: 4

FUEL: Thomas has enough puff to pull both of his carriages!

Once Emily took Thomas' carriages without asking. Thomas was very cross! No one told poor Emily that they were Thomas' coaches. Sometimes, when Thomas is busy, other engines help on Thomas' branch line. Annie and Clarabel don't mind being pulled by other Steamies, as long as they don't get a bumpy ride!

The Sodor Search and Rescue Centre is home to the Sodor Search and Rescue team. When the alarm sounds to signal an emergency on the Island, Harold, Flynn, Rocky, Belle, Butch or Captain will race to the rescue.

CAPTAIN
THE LIFEBOAT

PAINTWORK: Red, yellow, and blue with white stripes.

JOB: Sails Sodor's seas in search of anyone in danger.

ROCKY
THE RESCUE CRANE

PAINTWORK: Dark red and yellow.

JOB: Lifts engines back on to the rails with his strong crane arm.

Whether help is needed by rail, air, road or sea there's always a hero ready to save the day!

He looks tough but big Butch is a kind truck who helps anyone in trouble.

AUGMENTED REALITY

Get ready to fly Harold the Helicopter! Press the buttons to make Harold take off and land. Use the joystick to fly Harold around your room!

SODOR SEARCH AND RESCUE

SSRC

FLYNN
THE FIRE ENGINE

PAINTWORK: Fire-engine red!

JOB: Puts out fires with his powerful water cannons.

SEARCH RESCUE

Sir Bertram Topham Hatt, or The Fat Controller as his engines like to call him, is a friend to everyone on the Island of Sodor.

With engines and passengers to look after, timetables to write and freight to deliver, The Fat Controller is a very busy man!

Have you met The Fat Controller's family and friends?

Lady Hatt

Lady Jane Hatt is The Fat Controller's wife. She loves engines almost as much as her husband and often travels by train.

Dowager Hatt

Dowager Hatt is The Fat Controller's mother. She is always smartly dressed, in her green coat and hat.

Lowham Hatt

Sir Lowham Hatt is The Fat Controller's twin brother! They look very alike, except that Lowham has a black moustache.

The Earl of Sodor

Sir Robert Norramby is also known as the Earl of Sodor. Sir Robert travelled the world for many years before returning to Sodor.

The Thin Controller

Mr Percival is known as The Thin Controller. He controls the little engines on the Skarloey Railway.

DIESEL DUO

Paxton and Diesel may both be diesels but they couldn't be more different! Paxton loves to make friends wherever he goes, with Diesels and Steamies alike. But not many engines like working with devious Diesel!

Paxton backing into his berth at the Dieselworks.

Crafty Diesel is always up to his tricks!

DIESEL

PAINTWORK: Black with a red buffer beam.

WHEELS: 6

JOB: Shunting Troublesome Trucks in the Yard.

PAXTON

PAINTWORK: Dark green with red lining.

WHEELS: 6

JOB: Working in the Blue Mountain Quarry, carrying stone trucks to the Docks.

Thomas and his friends work very hard, but they know how to have fun, too! All the engines love parties, whether they are birthday, summer or winter celebrations!

Tidying List

ossible please carry on
at some point. Thank

Where you st

AUGMENTED REALITY

It's party time on Sodor! See if you can drive the trains to stop outside the station. Then celebrate with your friends!

The balloons make Brendam Docks look splendid!

Emily wears fairy lights in all different colours!

Bridget is Sir Topham's granddaughter. On her birthday, James was painted in only his undercoat. James felt very silly, but pink was Bridget's favourite colour!

Percy having fun at the Sodor Steamworks party.

THE BEST BUS

Although Thomas travels on a track and Bertie rides on roads, these two are still the best of friends!

BERTIE THE BUS

JOB: Bertie is a fine single-decker bus who brings passengers to Sodor's railway stations.

Once Bertie and Thomas decided to have a race to see who was faster. Thomas won the Great Race, but only just.

CREAKY CRANKY

Cranky is a tall crane who works down at the Docks. He doesn't make friends easily, as he is always so rude to the engines as they puff past him! Cranky can be kind, though . . .

JOB: Loading and unloading crates from the ships that arrive at the Docks.

Cranky is often grumpy because he works so hard – sometimes all day and all night. Cranky does have one friend – a seagull who likes to roost on his head! Cranky calls him Seagull!

Scruff and Whiff are the scruffiest and smelliest of all the engines on The Fat Controller's Railway. This grubby pair works together at Whiff's Waste Dump, shunting rubbish trucks and recycling rubbish so that it can be used again.

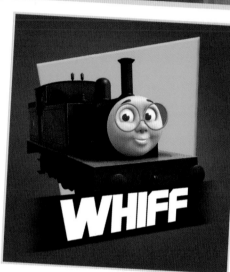

PAINTWORK: Dark green with black and gold lining.
WHEELS: 8
ENGINE TYPE: Tank engine.

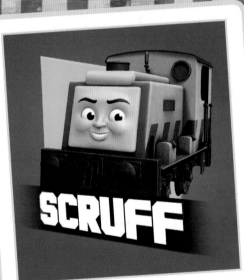

PAINTWORK: Lime green with dark green stripes.
WHEELS: 4
ENGINE TYPE: Sentinel steam shunter.

The engines like to look their best, but sometimes they have to do dirty jobs!

1

Here's Scruff being scrubbed from funnel to footplate. He wasn't very happy about it at first, but then he decided he liked feeling clean!

2

Once even The Fat Controller ended up wheel-deep in the mud! What a muddy mess!

3

Brave Belle is looking black and blue after helping to put out a fire at a farmhouse.

4

Spencer in the Steamworks wearing a splendid moustache made from soot!

5

The scruffiest engines on Sodor, Whiff and Scruff!

PUFFING PAIRS

Which engines on the Island of Sodor come as a pair? Follow the tracks to find two of a kind!

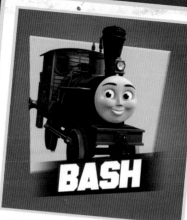

BASH

JOB: These twins were sent to work on Misty Island because they caused too much trouble on the Mainland!

BILL

JOB: Pulls trucks of China clay at the Quarry.

ARRY

JOB: One of a tricky pair who works at the scrapyards on Sodor.

CAITLIN

JOB: Brings passengers from the Mainland to visit Sodor.